WIN

with

Discipline

Ben Sillem

Illustrations by

Ali Imran

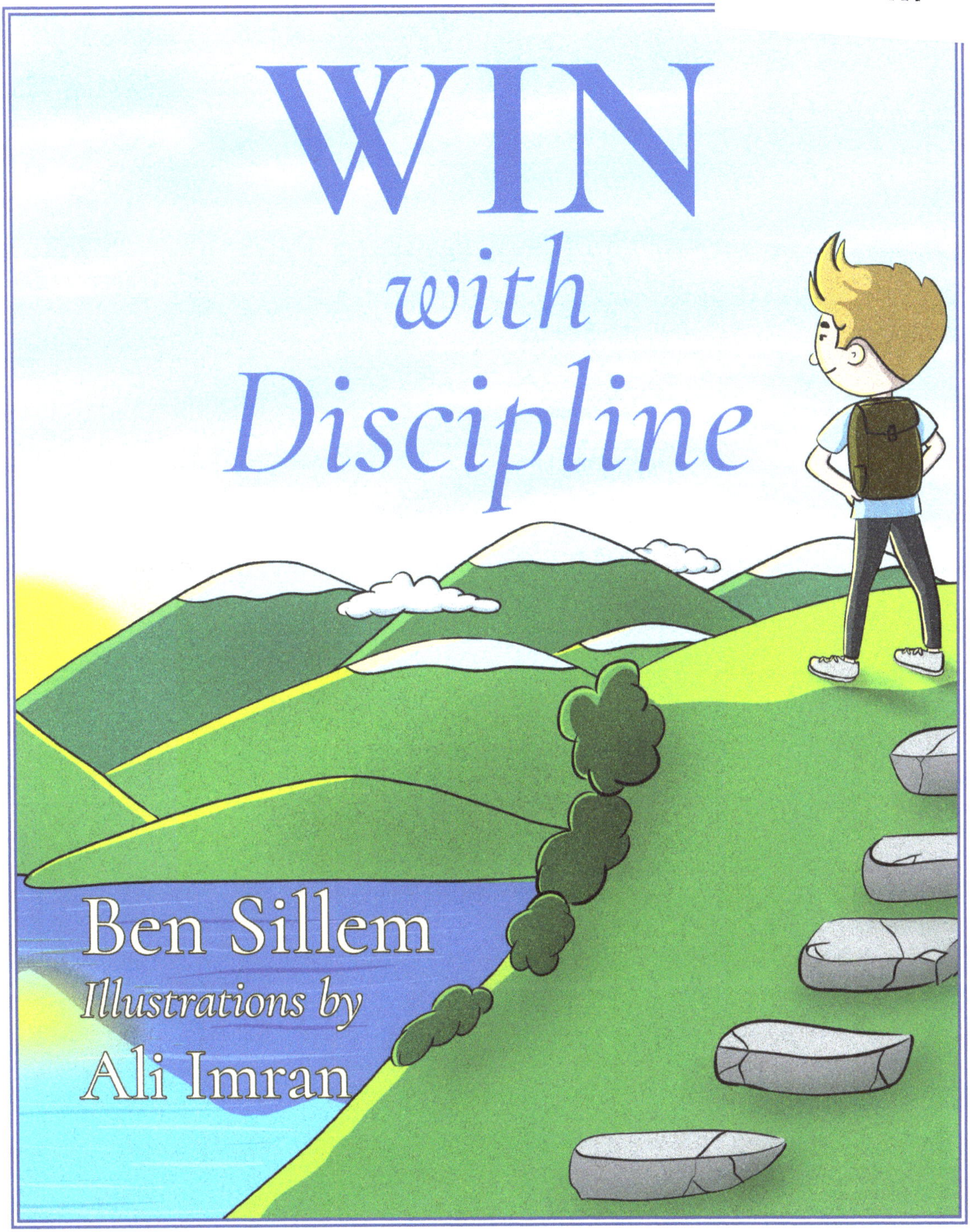

 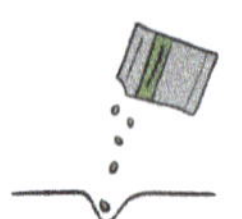   

Publisher: Ben Sillem
Contact: bsillem@brokerbuilder.ca

ISBN: 978-1-7782196-1-0 (softcover)
ISBN: 978-1-7782196-2-7 (eBook)

Illustrations by Ali Imran

Cover and page design, layout, and typesetting by
Jan Westendorp/katodesignandphoto.com

First Printing, 2022

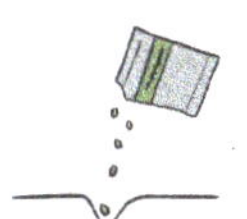

This book is dedicated to:

Those that do, and
Those that desire to
Delight in Discipline.

In other words, for you.

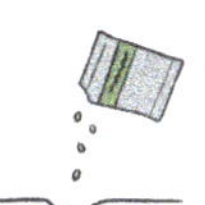

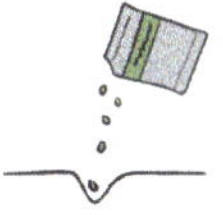

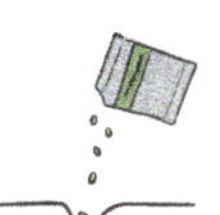

WIN

with

Discipline

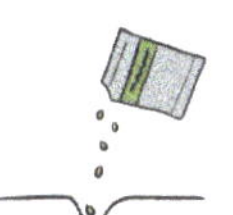

What is discipline?

It may be the difference maker.

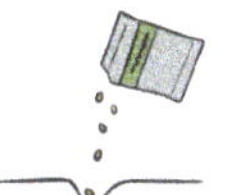

It's a giver, not a taker.

It's what will help you
become a mover and a shaker.

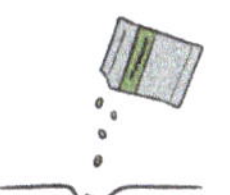

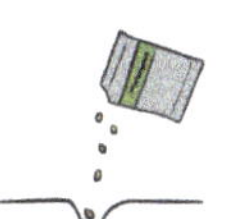

 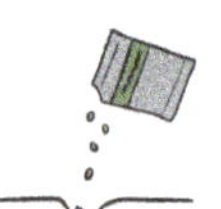   

Discipline is making choices in
which your future self rejoices.

 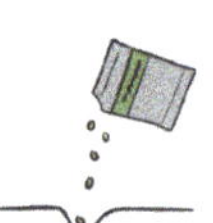

Everything in life that's nice,
carries with it some kind of price.

You can pay now, or
you can pay later.

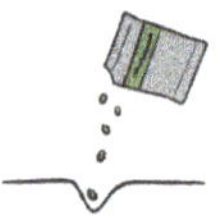 

The price in the future
will always be greater.

 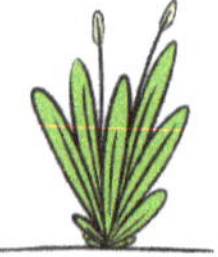

   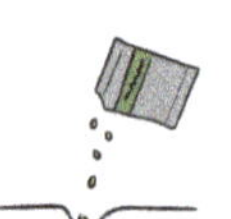 

Discipline is relenting,

From doing what is tempting.

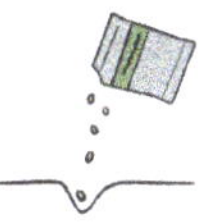

Passing on today's pleasure,

moves you closer to
tomorrow's treasure.

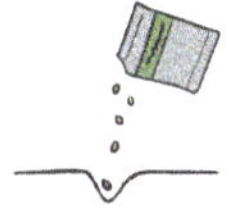

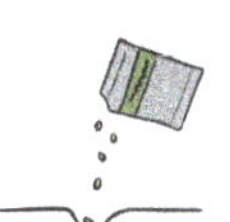

One marshmallow, two marshmallows,

three marshmallows, four.

If you're able to now ignore,

in the future all these you'll score.

If we believe in a brighter tomorrow,

then a sacrifice today is easier to swallow.

Bring near what you hold dear.

Make your goal vivid and clear.

Delight in Discipline,

It's your path to WIN.

Knowing **W**hat's **I**mportant **N**ow,

determines what you will allow.

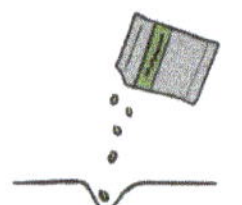

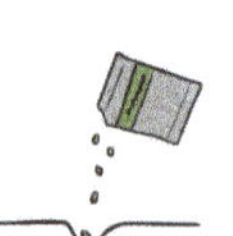

WIN

Do the things you need to do,

in order to yourself stay true.

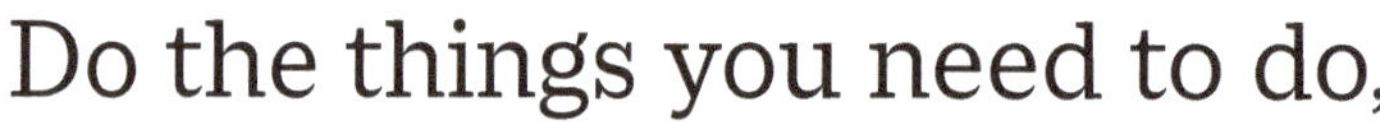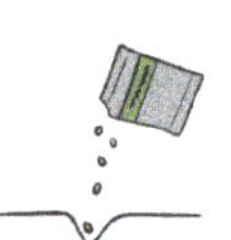

Instead of being driven by desires,

become someone that inspires.

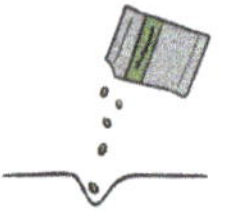

Can you see future you?

Do you have a concept of
what you want as a view?

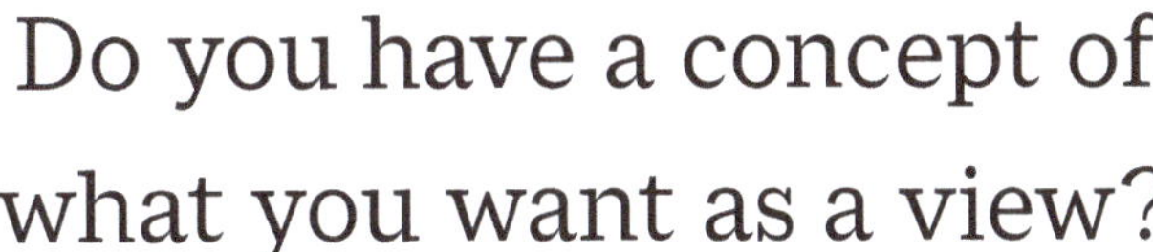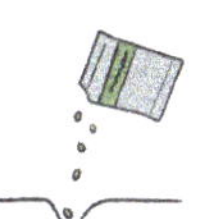

When you know where
you're trying to go,

A path of steps will begin to show.

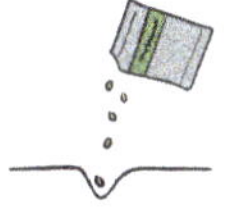

unhealthy
LOSE

healthy
MIN

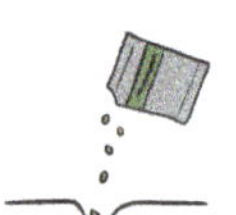

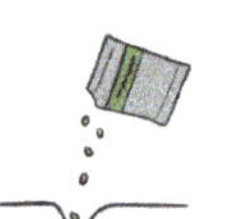

With each choice we make,

One of two paths we take.

One serves, the other stifles.
Each decision, therefore, is not trifle.

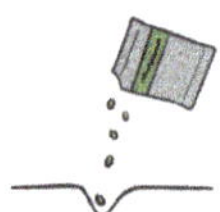

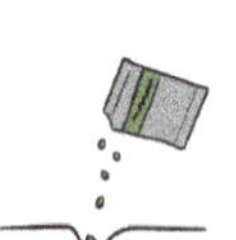

Genetics and heredity,

Aren't all that make up you and me.

We can become
what we dream to be.

If we use discipline to
develop our ability.

Do something now
that will serve you later.

Over time, you will become greater.

So, get up and get going.

Soon your skill will be growing.

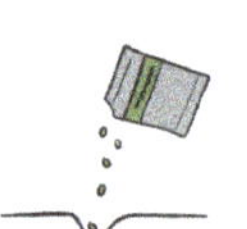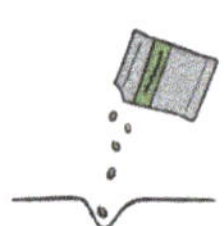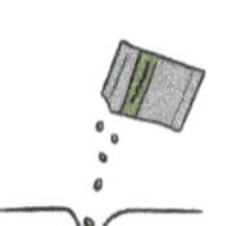

Find your rhythm, feel your beat,

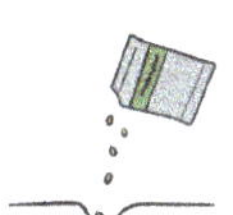

with sound daily
practices you can repeat.

Step by step, with your two feet,

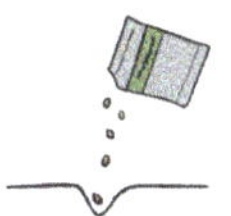

your dreams and goals you will meet.

D
I
S
C
I
P

L
L I N E
I
21

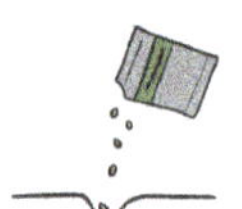

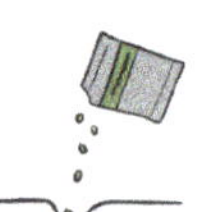

Discipline isn't one and done.

It's hard work and never won.

Step on the path,

and embrace the math.

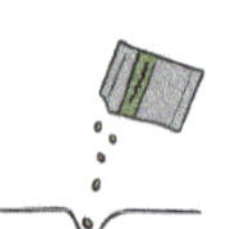

This much is certainly true,

Here's a thought to let brew.

Daily what you duly do

Defines who it is are you.

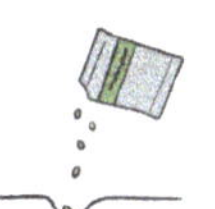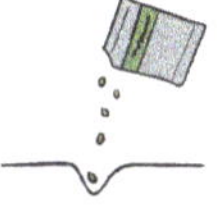

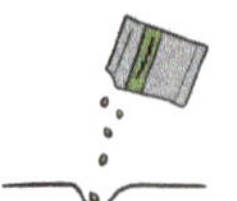

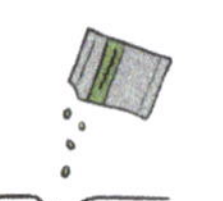

Drip by drip,

just don't quit.

Bit by bit,

you become legit.

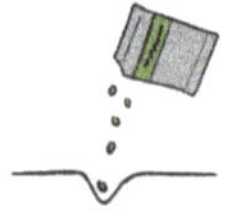

Discipline is nothing new.

 It was and is what's good for you. 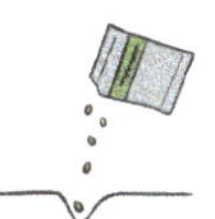

 Do what you need to do before
what you want to do, 

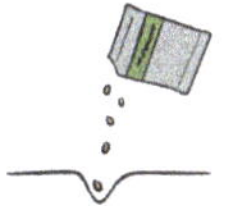 and in this world, there
will always be a place for you. 

   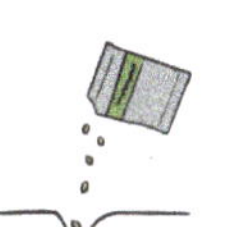 

Change is hard and that's ok.

Do the work anyway.

Put in the effort every day.

Discipline becomes a game to play.

WIN with Discipline
HEALTH
EDUCATION

 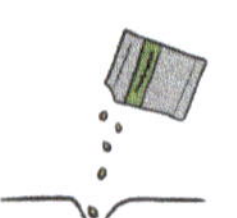   

Doing discipline makes
it part of your skin.

 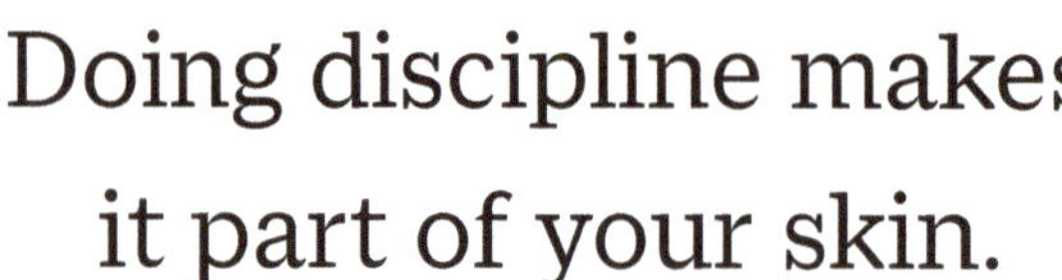 

It helps you forever get
through thick and thin.

 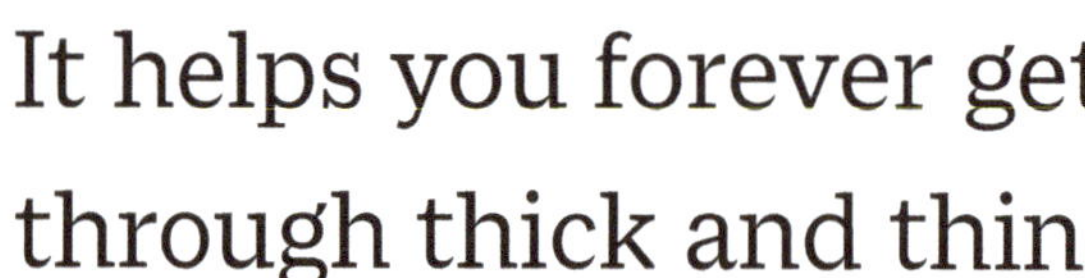 

With each small act of discipline,

You can claim a personal win.

Embracing discipline
puts you in charge,

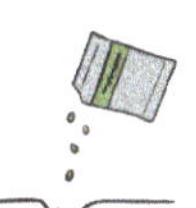

Of living a life that will be large.

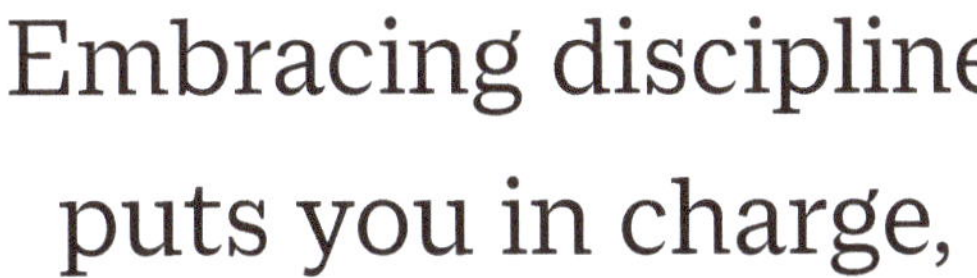

With discipline build
routines that rhyme,

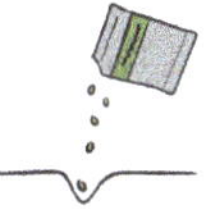

Recognizing that
good things take time.

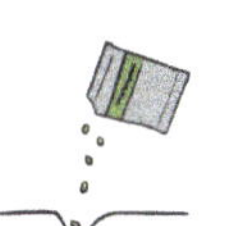

If you're all about play,

Further from your
desired target you'll stray.

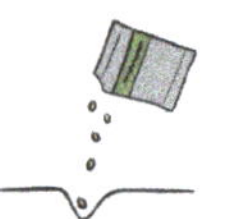

The more we delay,
the more we decay.

A lack of discipline is
a heavy price to pay.

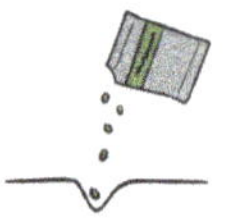

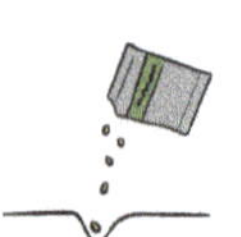

VR
CHIPS
CHOC
CHOC
CHOC
CHOC

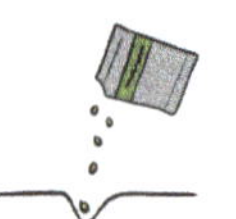

There's little that can be gained,

If we run from each little pain.

Our future's more likely to be bleak,

Where we let our discipline leak.

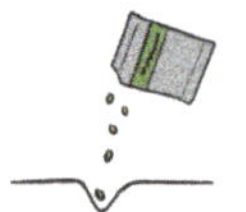

To avoid a life of flirting with disaster,

Of yourself you must
become a master.

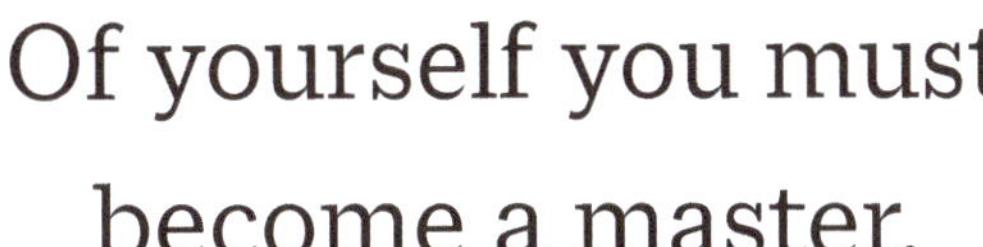

You'll know a good day it has been.

When you've done
some acts of discipline.

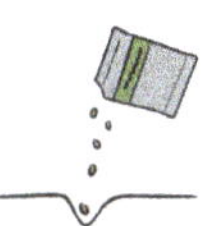

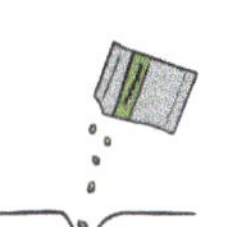

With discipline you'll learn to revel,

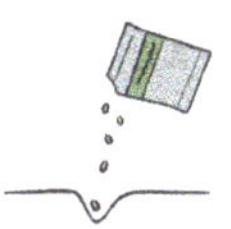

In a battle with your inner devil.

Daily discipline deletes doubt,

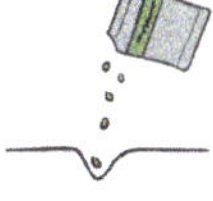

And provides evidence
of your growing clout.

We can get better or end up bitter.

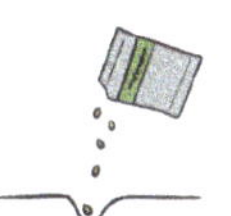

Choose to serve in order to deserve.

Give now to get later.

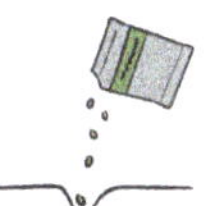

It's the surest way
to becoming greater.

Get a good night sleep.
Watch what you eat.

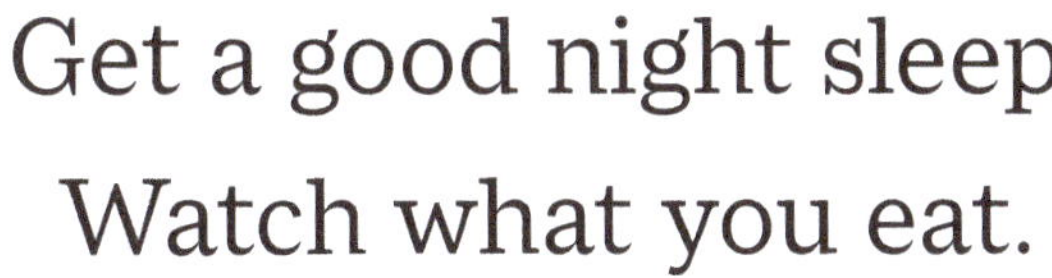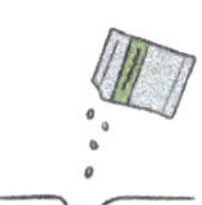

Try to become wise and
find time to exercise.

Hold your tongue and get some sun.

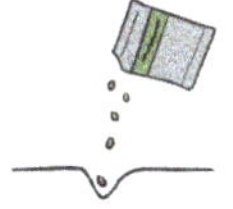With discipline, your life's more fun.

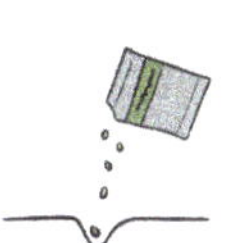

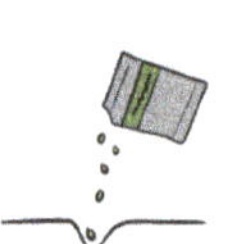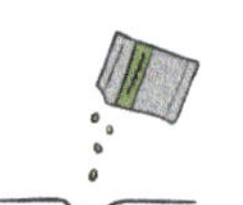

Discipline is steady fuel.

It's your most valuable tool.

Hold on to it like a precious jewel.

With it yourself you'll rule.

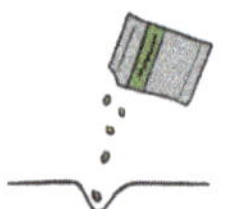

DISCIPLINE
is the KEY to me
DISCIPLINE

The best way to roll,

Is with self-control.

With discipline in your hands,

42

There won't be much
outside your command.

Discipline is paying attention
and taking notes,

Instead of doodling
and telling jokes.

You Can't be great while being late
Discipline helps you get out of the gate

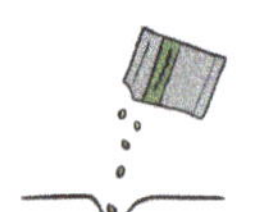

If there's one thing useful to learn,

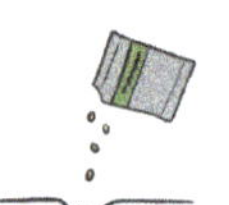

It's success is
something we must earn.

Discipline allows you
to overcome resistance,

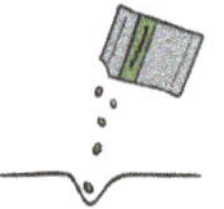

And patiently
pursue with persistence.

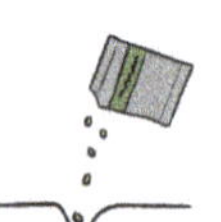

There's no feat you can't complete.

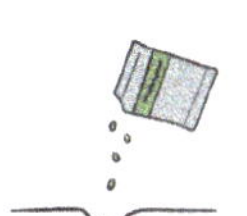

In due time, your
objectives you'll meet.

Learn to say you'll chip away,

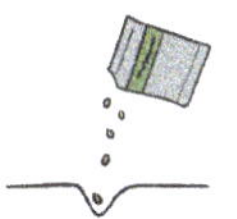

Not just today, but every day.

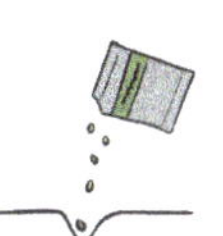

Say goodbye to shortcuts,
lotto tickets, big breaks, and hacks.

Count on discipline to have your back.

48

Of discipline become a disciple.

Depend on it as your core principle.

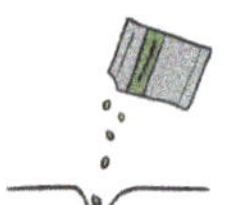

Discipline isn't giving up what's nice.

It's not all struggle and sacrifice.

It's patience, temperance,
and moderation,

All imply your participation.

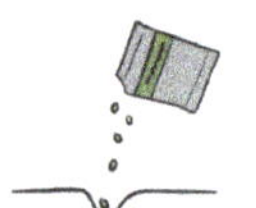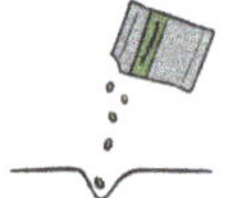

On discipline you can depend,

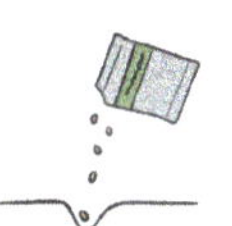

To be a loyal and helpful friend.

Add discipline to your core creed.

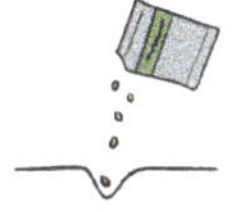

You can count on it to
provide what you need.

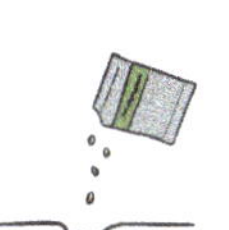

Put the I in discipline.

Make it a part of you.

Do the do,

and earn your view.

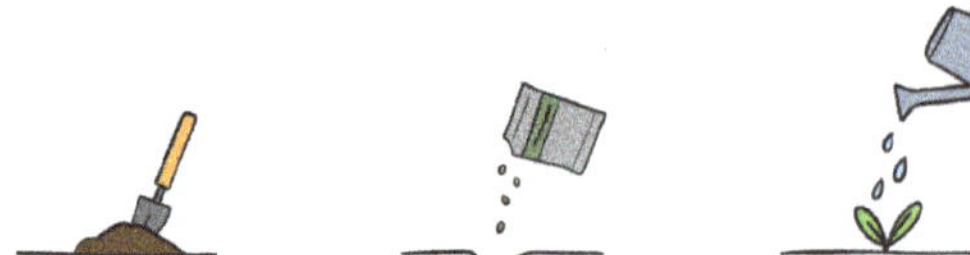

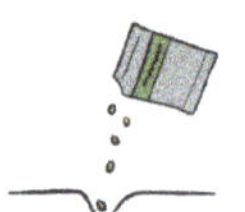

The End

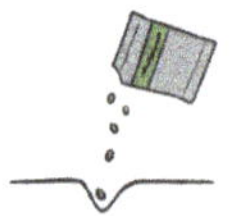

Where's Joey headed next?

Coming soon: Join Joey
on his next adventure
as he leans in to learning
by cultivating curiosity.

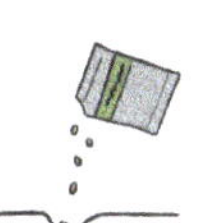